WINTER KILL

A Clay Jared Western

R. Annan

Winter Kill
Copyright 2016 by R. Annan
E. 1.1
WGA Reg. #: R31722 (02.09.16)

Author's Portrait by Hazel Tertsakian
Editor: Karren Doll Tolliver
Photography © L. Annan

One Vision Publishing
ISBN: 978-1-942338-52-9 (eBook)
ISBN: 978-1-942338-51-2 (Print)

Other western books by R. Annan:

Fight for the Lazy M
The Gunfighter in Winter
Long Ride to Hell's Kitchen
Owl Hawks
Gunfight at Barfield Springs
Shootout at Sanctuary City
Last Days of a Gunfighter
The Red Bandana
Copperhead Moon
Cowboys of the Box R
Prisoners of Brimstone Pass
Range War in C Minor
Devil Wind
Showdown at Wamego Falls
Lightning Riders

Dedicated To

Hazel Tertsakian

A good friend and artist

1.

Clay Jared was two days west of Stockton when the temperature dropped and it began to snow hard. In a few minutes he couldn't see more than ten feet ahead. The road he was following quickly disappeared under a blanket of snow.

He knew he should have turned back, but he was too tired and kept going. Suddenly, without warning, the horse went sliding on its hindquarters down a steep bank into a gully surrounded by pine trees. Jared was tossed from the saddle as both man and animal fought for control.

Once at the bottom Jared got up and brushed the snow off his clothing. His mount whinnied and struggled to its feet. It stared at Jared looking confused. Jared chuckled, patted its neck and climbed back into the saddle.

Jared decided to ride along the gully instead of trying to climb up the steep grade to the top. He hoped it would even out somewhere ahead. Regardless, it was snowing so hard he couldn't see where the top was. The wind was whipping the snow around in blinding sheets.

A hundred yards ahead, Jared ran into a stand of birch trees. It opened out into a level strip of land bordered by a rock cliff on his left and more birches on his right. It was here he saw an orange glow in the distance and headed straight for it. As he got closer he saw a crude campsite under the rocky overhang of a cliff. There was a stream nearby that had a thin crust of ice on it.

Three hatless men wrapped in dark green blankets stood around a fire cooking a skinned rabbit on a stick. They had their backs to him, and, because of the howling wind, never heard him coming.

"Hello," Jared yelled from twenty feet away. They quickly turned to stare at him.

"Come on in," the leader, a tall man with broad shoulders, yelled back against the force of the wind.

Jared dismounted, tied his horse to a tree and made his way through the snow to the shelter of the overhang. After stomping the snow off his boots and brushing himself down, he got close to the fire and held his hands over it to warm them.

"I'm lost," Jared said. "How do I get back on the road to Stockton?"

The other two men, one chubby and one thin, walked slowly up on each side of him. The big one stood on the other side of the fire, grinning.

Jared suddenly realized he had blundered into the camp of three cutthroats.

"You ain't goin' to Stockton, cowboy," the big man growled.

He dropped his blanket and Jared saw he was wearing a filthy, ragged prison uniform.

As Jared made a move in the direction of his horse, the two men beside him grabbed his arms and held him fast. The big one came over and clubbed him in the jaw with a huge fist. Jared groaned and his knees buckled. As he fell, another blow sent him into a silent, black world.

When he came to, it was night and he was lying in the snow. His body shook and he felt the stabbing pain of the cold as it ran through his body. He quickly realized he was naked except for his flannel underwear. They had taken all

3

his other clothes, even his socks, hat and boots. The side of his face was sore and swollen where the bruiser had hit him.

Jared forced himself to stand up in the snow on his bare feet. A second later his body began to shake violently. The fire was almost out. He noticed a pile of branches nearby and tossed some on the embers. In a few moments a breeze came along and the flames flared up. Jared jumped around and slapped his arms against his body to get the circulation going. It didn't help, and he realized he was going to freeze to death. In half an hour he would be dead.

That's when he saw the dirty, old prison blanket on the ground. Most likely one of the convicts had discarded it for Jared's clothing. He quickly picked it up, spread it open and held it above the fire to warm it. Moments later he wrapped it around his back and shoulders, then hunkered up close to the fire. The rock floor by the fire felt warm to his feet.

He hunched there alone, close to the flames, wondering when daylight would come. Once or twice he nodded off and almost fell into the fire. The darkness seemed to go on forever. At last he saw the first hint of dawn. By then all the wood from the pile had been used up and he was cold again.

He quickly tore two wide and two thin strips from the blanket. Winding the wide strips about his feet, he tied them fast with the thin strips. He tried walking. They felt good.

Tearing another wide and thin strip, he set them aside and looked for a rock with a sharp edge. When he found one he used it to cut a slit in the center of the leftover piece of blanket, a slit long enough to slip his head through, thereby making a crude serape long enough to hang down over his thighs. He used the last thin strip to tie the blanket around his waist. Jared was glad they hadn't taken his red flannel underwear. He was feeling warmer already.

Before leaving, Jared got a rock the size of his fist and tied it up in the remaining wide strip of blanket so that he could whirl it about like a weapon. After breaking the ice on the stream and drinking, he left at a slow run, following the tracks in the snow.

It wasn't long before he had to slow down and grab his side in pain. He panted for air but it was so cold it burned his lungs. Finally, he stopped to rest. Five minutes later he struggled on again. It went like that, stopping and starting, for about an hour before he saw a dark object up ahead. The snow was falling fast and he wasn't sure what it was.

Suddenly it moved. It was the short, stocky convict. He saw Jared coming and stood waiting to do battle. Jared closed with him and swung the rock against the left side of his head. There was a sickening, bone-crushing sound as the rock smashed the convict's skull, driving him sideways until he landed in a twisted heap in the snow.

Jared quickly glanced down once as he ran past the body.

Turning a curve in the trail, he saw the big convict and his smaller partner tangled up in a struggle. The big one pulled the boot knife from Jared's boots he was wearing and stabbed his companion several times in the chest, leaving him dead on the ground.

Then he turned to face Jared and waited, the bloody knife out and ready.

"Come an' git it, cowboy," the convict bellowed angrily.

"You first," Jared yelled above the wind.

The big man made a lunge for Jared.

Jared swung the rock once and broke the man's jaw. As the convict stood stunned, Jared whirled around like a dancer and delivered a second blow that caved in the convict's forehead. The big man dropped like a fallen tree into the snow.

The cowboy stood stooped over, panting from exertion. His horse came over and nuzzled him. Jared put an arm around its neck and hung on for a moment.

"Thanks, pal," he said.

He got out his canteen, drank and then got some jerky from the saddlebag. It was frozen hard but he managed to chew a few bites, enough to revive him.

The big convict was wearing Jared's clothes and gunbelt. Jared struggled to get them off him and onto himself. Dressed against the cold again, he felt better. As he started to leave, he noticed the rock, walked over and untied it from the strip of blanket and put it in his saddlebag. It had saved his life and was worth keeping. It had a story to tell.

Mounting up, Jared rode slowly along the strip of hardpan between the wall of rocks and the trees. In about half an hour it opened into a downgrade that looked upon a wide vista below. The snow had slacked off and he saw a wagon train and people about a hundred yards down the slope.

He sat there watching them in the afterglow of the westering sun, exhausted and lost.

2.

Jared couldn't make out what kind of wagons they were. There were four of them and they all had long, flat beds piled high with something hidden under canvas tarps. Each wagon was pulled by a team of two horses and had two people in the driver's box.

As the wagons came alongside a stand of pine trees on the right, gunfire erupted and riders rushed out, shooting into the caravan. Jared counted at least five. It all happened very quickly. They attacked the wagons, killed the drivers and set fire to the cargo. Whatever was on the wagons burned easily and quickly.

The marauders hit hard and fast and then were gone back into the trees. Jared watched them pass through the pines, over a rise and out of sight. The wagon train had been caught by surprise. The men who had attacked it were good at what they did. They hadn't lost a single man in the raid.

By the time Jared got down to the bottom of the long slope, flames were shooting high into the sky, whipped by the wind and lighting up the night. He saw bales of hay exploding into flames and could feel the heat from thirty feet away. Riding around the wagons, Jared stared at the dead bodies. Some of the drivers had died on their seats and were being cooked by the flames. Jared caught the scent of burning flesh.

Other drivers lay sprawled on the ground. The snow was already covering their bodies with a blanket of white. The redness of their blood stood out against the whiteness of the snow.

Suddenly one team of horses, terrified by the flames, ran off into the field, spilling their load and leaving a trail of blazing hay and grain behind them. Jared quickly dismounted, got out his boot knife and cut the other three teams loose. They ran for the open field to escape the heat.

Jared could now see that the cargo really was bales of hay and sacks of grain. The sacks exploded as the flames consumed them, sending burning grain shooting high and flying off into the fields. The hay crackled and spit out sparks that were picked up and carried by the wind.

Jared walked carefully around the scene of destruction to see if anyone was alive. As he went down the line checking, he heard a human sound, a moan that was carried to him on the wind. He stopped, looked in its direction and saw a man on his face in the snow, trying to get up. Jared ran to him and turned him slowly over.

It turned out to be a young girl of about eighteen or nineteen, dressed in men's clothing. She was shot in the right side and was bleeding badly.

She looked up at Jared and smiled weakly.

"Hi, handsome."

Jared unbuckled her gunbelt, stuffed it quickly into his saddlebag and lifted her up onto his saddle rise.

"Grab the apple," he said. She grabbed the saddle horn and Jared swung up beside her. He turned his horse and started off at a fast gait down the road.

"Who are you, mister?"

"Don't talk," Jared said.

She leaned back between his arms. It seemed like a long time before he saw a sign that read Kherson's Flats and soon after that a small town where smoke rose from the chimneys of frame houses.

He approached on the back end of town where the stable

was. A man came out of a small shack to greet him.

"I need a doctor!"

For a moment the man was confused.

"Doc Edmunds, fifty feet up the road into town," the man stammered, spitting a stream of brown chewing tobacco into the snow. "But he ain't there."

"Where the hell is he?"

"He's in the Double Down Saloon drinkin' an' playin' poker, is where he is. Everybody knows thet!"

"Jesus!" Jared muttered and nudged his horse up the road.

He passed the sign over the doctor's place and finally came to the Double Down Saloon. Sliding out of the saddle, he lifted the girl carefully down into his arms and carried her up onto the porch and through the batwing doors.

As he stepped in, a piano stopped playing in the back and the place went quiet. Everyone stared at Jared and the girl.

The barman took one look and yelled, "God Almighty! Doc!"

"Over here!" a crusty old voice said calmly.

Jared carried the woman over and laid her on the poker table, scattering the cards and money.

"Christ! It's Shelly Kincaid!" one of the players yelled.

"Get my bag, Tom!" an old, white-haired man said.

The barman rushed over with the doctor's bag and handed it to the scruffy old man with long white hair who was dressed in a worn wool suit. The old man dropped his half-smoked cigar on the floor, struggled out of his coat and rolled up his shirt sleeves.

"Tom, get me some hot water, please, and some clean towels," the doctor said as he opened his bag.

A man in a suit who looked like a businessman walked up alongside Jared. Others joined him.

"Who did this, mister?" the man asked sadly.

Before Jared could answer, a marshal came in the door brushing snow off his coat. He was older than the doctor, a bit stooped over at the shoulders and thin as a pole.

"What's goin' on?" the marshal asked.

"Ask this fellah," someone answered. "He just carried

Shelly Kincaid in, all shot up!"

The marshal walked up to Jared.

"I'm Marshal Richards. Ted Fields down at the stables said you brought Shelly in. What happened to her?"

"She was with four wagons that got shot up and burned west of town, about half an hour ago," Jared said. "There's a bunch of dead men out there. Some are probably burnt to a cinder by now."

"Jesus, Mary and Joseph!" Tom, the barman gasped.

"Who is she?" Jared asked.

"She's Shelly Kincaid, daughter of Frank Kincaid," the marshal said. "When he hears about this there's gonna be hell ta pay." The old marshal sighed big. "I'd better get a posse together and ride out there. You had best come along, too."

"Alright, sure. I'll wait here. Let me know when you're ready to go."

After the marshal left, Jared walked over to the table and stood there watching the doctor as he bent over the body of Shelly Kincaid.

"Stay awake, girl! Don't you quit on me, baby! I brought

you into this world and you ain't leavin' it before I do!"

The barman said something to Jared. At first he didn't hear, but then said, "I'll have a beer. Any kind, so long as it's wet." He grabbed a pickled hardboiled egg from a jar and swallowed it in two bites. He grabbed another and a piece of jerky and devoured them also.

"Jesus," the barman said. "You must be half starved."

Jared nodded and got a pickled cucumber and a piece of hardtack from the bar offerings and quickly dispatched them, too. He followed that with half of the bottle of beer. He tossed a double eagle on the bar and said to keep the change.

A cowboy came over to the bar and nodded at the barman.

"I'm gonna ride out to the Double K and tell Ol' Man Kincaid what happened."

"Good idea," the barman said, and the cowboy left.

Another cowboy came over, this time to talk to Jared.

"She's asking fer you, cowboy."

Jared shrugged and followed the cowboy over to where Shelly Kincaid lay on the poker table. She had a bandage around her waist below her rib cage.

15

"How is she, Doc?" Jared asked.

"The bullet went clean through. Barely missed her liver. She's lucky," the doctor said. He turned to the girl. "You'd best take it easy for a week or two, girl."

Shelly Kincaid wasn't listening to the doctor. She was staring at Jared.

"Come here, cowboy," she said. It was an order.

Jared walked over beside her. Shelly reached up, grabbed his coat, pulled him down and kissed him on the lips. After doing that, she fainted.

3.

An hour later Jared joined the posse and rode out to where the ambush had happened. They had a buckboard with them. When they got there, the wagons were still burning. The marshal sent two men to round up the horses.

"Ol' Kincaid is gonna be mighty pissed off," the marshal said.

It started to snow harder but it didn't seem to dampen the blazing cargo.

"Load the bodies on the buckboard, boys," the marshal yelled.

"What about those thet's burnin'?" someone yelled back.

"If ya can't put the fire out, let 'em burn. We'll come back out in the mornin' and clean up this mess."

"Shouldn't we go after them bastards?" another asked.

"It's too dark ta see anything," the marshal said. "We'll have to wait for mornin'. We can't do anything tonight."

"It's gettin' colder!" someone complained.

Jared moved his horse up closer to the marshal. "Say, Marshal, was there a prison break around here lately?"

"Yeah, three men busted out of the county jail. They was slated ta hang, but killed a guard and busted out."

"They're all dead," Jared said. "I killed them today, back up there in the woods."

"All three?" the marshal asked as if he didn't believe it.

"Yep, all three."

"Can you show me the bodies?"

"Sure."

"There's a five hundred-dollar reward for each one," the marshal said. "We'll go out there as soon as possible and bring the bodies in." He stared at Jared. "Boy, you're plumb lucky ta be alive. Them was rapists and killers, all three of 'em."

Later they rode alongside the buckboard carrying four unburnt bodies. They were a mile from Kherson's Flats when a man in a one-horse buckboard came up behind them and waved the marshal down. All three stopped while the rest went on towards town.

"Howdy, Frank," the marshal said.

Frank Kincaid was a big man. He had long, unkempt hair streaked with white under his black Stetson and a full beard to match the hair. He resembled a hell-fire-damnation preacher more than he resembled a rancher.

"How many, Fred?" Kincaid asked the marshal.

"All of 'em."

"Oh, God, not Shelly!"

"No, but she got shot bad. Lucky fer her this young man came along. He brung her in and the doc took care of her. If it hadn't a been fer him, she'd be dead, Frank."

Kincaid stared hard at Jared, sizing him up good.

"Ride with me, son," Kincaid said. It was a command. Jared tied his horse to the buckboard and climbed up alongside the rancher. Kincaid handed him the reins. Jared got the buckboard moving towards town.

"Tell me what happened."

Jared told what he had seen. The old man listened and nodded.

"She's my granddaughter. She's the last of the Kincaids,

after me. I'm grateful to you fer savin' her."

"Who'd want to burn your grain shipment, Mr. Kincaid?"

"I don't know," the rancher said. He paused a moment, then said, "Whoever they were, they did a good job. There won't be any more."

"Why not?"

"Because it'll only happen agin an' I'll end up with no grain, a lot of dead men and owing the bank money I can't pay back."

"I see."

"Hell, I ain't the only one in trouble. This is gonna be a bad winter an' the other ranchers are in the same boat as I am."

They rode into Kherson's Flats and tied up at the Double Down Saloon. Marshal Richards rode up alongside them.

"I'll take the bodies over to the undertakers, Frank."

"Alright, Fred, thanks."

The posse and the buckboard moved on. Jared and the old rancher went into the saloon. Shelly Kincaid was sitting up in a chair looking pale and tired.

An overweight man of about fifty years old wearing a fur coat stood looking down at her. He held a fedora in one hand and had the other hand on Shelly's shoulder. His coal-black hair was slicked back flat on his small head. A pencil-thin mustache adorned his mouth above fat, puckered-up lips.

When Jared and her grandfather walked in, Shelly Kincaid looked at them and smiled, ignoring the man.

"Hi, Gran'pa!" she said, trying to sound energetic.

Frank Kincaid went to his granddaughter and stood looking down at her with a concerned look.

"Are you alright, girl?"

"I'm fine, Gran'pa."

"Hello, Frank," the man said.

"Hello, Mr. Talbert," Kincaid said. The man reached over and grabbed the old rancher's hand and shook it.

"Frank," Talbert said, "I've made arrangements for Shelly to stay at Ma Bradley's boarding house until she's well enough to travel. But she wants to make that long ride back to the Double K. Perhaps you can talk some sense into her."

"Better listen to Mr. Talbert, girl," the old rancher said seriously. "You look like a ghost. You need a week in bed." Frank Kincaid turned to Jared. "Mr. Talbert, this is the young man who found Shelly and saved her life."

Talbert looked at Jared with raised eyebrows and gave him a weak smile. There was instant dislike in that look.

"I'm very thankful, young man," Talbert said, almost as if dismissing a servant. He turned to Kincaid. "I'll get my carryall and take Shelly over to Ma Bradley's place."

He smiled down at Shelly for a moment, gave Jared a blank stare and left.

Jared chuckled. "Who's that?"

"Greg Talbert. He manages the Kherson's Flats Savings and Loan," Kincaid said. "He has a small real estate business here in town, too."

Jared nodded. "Important man in town, huh?"

"Yeah," Kincaid said. He chuckled, "And he's asked Shelly to marry him."

"Three times," Shelly said.

"Oh?" Jared chuckled. "What's holding you back?"

"I'm still thinking on it." She stared at Jared. "Anyway, he's kinda old."

Old Kincaid shook his head. "Well, you won't get a better offer here in this town, girl."

"Maybe, maybe not." Shelly said. She never took her eyes off Jared.

Talbert came back with his small, one-horse coach. Jared picked Shelly up, carried her out and set her in it.

"I can handle it from here," Talbert said sharply.

He got in the coach beside Shelly, snapped the reins and drove away. Kincaid motioned for Jared to follow him back into the saloon. They had a drink at the bar.

"Where are you from, Jared?"

"Fifty miles south. The Flying R."

"Never heard of it."

The marshal came in and joined them at the bar.

"This place sure is dead for a Friday, Tom," the marshal said.

"It's the weather, Marshal," Tom said.

Jared noticed that old Doc Edmunds had gone back to playing poker as if nothing had happened.

"Have a drink, Marshal?" Kincaid asked.

"Just one, Frank. Just ta warm my insides. It's gettin' real cold out there."

Kincaid looked at Jared. "What's your plans for the night, Jared?"

"I guess I'll bed my horse down at the stables and find a place to sleep."

"Come on over to the jailhouse," the marshal said. "There's two empty cots there. You take one an' I'll take the other. There's plenty of blankets."

Jared smiled. "Sounds pretty good to me, Marshal."

"In the morning we'll go get them bodies."

That remark caught Kincaid's attention.

"Bodies? What bodies?"

"Jared says he kilt those three murderers who broke outta the county jail."

Kincaid stared at Jared. "Jesus! You sure were busy today, Jared."

The marshal chuckled. "That's what I first said, too, Frank."

"Are you a bounty hunter, Jared?" Kincaid asked.

"No."

"So, how did it happen?"

"I got lost and ran into them up in the hills. They tried to kill me."

"An you ended up killing them?" Kincaid asked.

"That's about it." Jared replied.

"You're either good or you're lucky," Kincaid replied. He yawned. "Well, I'm goin' over to Ma Bradley's and get a room for the night. It's too damn cold ta ride all the way back to the Double K. I'll check on Shelly while I'm there."

"Give her my regards," Jared said.

"I'll do that." Kincaid stood up to leave, then hesitated. He turned to Jared. "If yer lookin' for a lousy job with low pay but good food, come see me at the Double K, Jared."

"I'll sleep on it, Mr. Kincaid," Jared said.

"If them cheap asses on the town council would let me hire a deputy, I'd hire you myself," the marshal said.

After Kincaid left, Jared and the marshal did, too. The cowboy walked his horse down to the stables, stripped off its gear, then fed and watered it. Finally, he laid a blanket over its back, spoke softly to it and walked back to the jailhouse. The marshal had churned up the fire in the potbelly stove and had gotten the chill out of the room.

They talked a while then turned in for the night, leaving the oil lamp burning but the door bolted.

As he lay on the cot in the cell, Jared recalled the softness of Shelly Kincaid's lips.

4.

After taking Shelly Kincaid to Ma Bradley's boarding house, Greg Talbert parked his coach behind his real estate business and entered through the back door to his private quarters. It was where he slept and made his plans and did his scheming. As for the real estate business, Talbert only opened it on Saturdays. During the weekdays he managed the bank. Sundays were free for socializing about town.

He sat at his desk by the light of an oil lamp and waited. In half an hour a man opened the door, letting in a blast of cold air and snow. He quickly slammed it shut and brushed the white stuff from his coat and hat.

The man was a few years older than Talbert, but was tall and broad-shouldered compared to Talbert's short pudginess. The man could have been mistaken for a boxer. He didn't look like the average citizen of Kherson's Flats, and in fact he wasn't. Everyone in town knew him as the man who stood guard at the bank. His name was Art Flynn. Five days a week they expected him to greet them at the entrance of the

Cattlemen's Savings and Loan Bank, where Talbert was the manager.

Flynn idolized his boss and would do almost anything for him, including hiring a bunch of drifters, cutthroats and bums from a nearby cattle town to raid the Kincaid grain caravan and kill its drivers. All for twenty bucks each, a month's wages for a hard working cowboy. It wasn't much to Talbert, but it was a lot to them.

While Talbert had lots of money, there was one thing he didn't yet have, and that was Shelly Kincaid. He had wanted her since he first set his beady black eyes on her. She was a wild, free spirit of the West, always beyond his grasp, dancing like a butterfly on the wind, back and forth, now within grasp, now too far to touch.

But after tonight she was almost within reach.

"You almost had her killed!" Talbert yelled at Flynn.

"Who, boss?"

"Shelly Kincaid! She was with the wagon train!"

Flynn shrugged.

"Hell, how was I supposed ta know? Anyway, the old man never shoulda let her go. He shoulda kept her at home!"

"But he didn't! And she was shot bad!"

Talbert sighed and settled down. He got a bottle of whiskey and two glasses from the big bottom drawer of his desk, poured two drinks and handed one to Flynn.

The banker stared at Flynn. "Outside of her getting hurt, you did a nice job, Flynn. I think I've got the old fool right where I want him."

Flynn got out the makings and started to build a cigarette. "You think so?"

"Yes," Talbert said. "He'll come to the bank for a loan. I'm certain of it. He has no choice now."

"Will you give it to him, boss?" Flynn asked.

"Perhaps, or maybe I'll just refuse and turn him down flat. Tell him he's a bad risk. Once I got him worried I'll go out there and pay the two of them a visit. I'll bet she'll treat me with more respect then."

"Looks like you've got them at yer mercy, boss. Right in the palm of yer hands!" Flynn chuckled.

"She won't turn me down the next time, I'm sure. She'll know now it's the only way to save the Double K."

Flynn finished rolling his cigarette and lit it.

"Where'd you get all yer money, boss?"

"Smart investments, Flynn," Talbert said. "Some people know how to make money the easy way, and some work their fingers to the bone for pennies. Like those stupid cowboys you used tonight."

"What's so important that you want the Double K spread, boss?"

"Because I've never owned a ranch."

"Hell, is that all?"

"If I own a ranch, Flynn, I become one of them, you see."

Flynn chuckled.

"You gonna make me foreman?"

"Ranches don't have foremen, Flynn, they have ramrods."

"Ramrods?" Flynn repeated, "Ramrod Flynn. I like the sound of it. Yer damn smart, boss, damn smart."

Talbert smiled. "Yes, I am. And once I own the Double K Ranch maybe I'll propose to the Kansas Pacific that they run a trunk line through the center of it, connecting

Kherson's Flats with Newton."

"Why would they do that?" Flynn asked.

"Because it's cattle country all the way south. They could connect Salina with Herington, Lindsey, Hillsboro, Peabody and Newton. All in one straight line."

Flynn chuckled. "Yer a genius, boss!"

"Of course I am, Flynn. After all, I took a course in real estate, too, you know," Talbert said. "Of course I'm smart." He poured them both another drink. "It's all about money, my friend. Never forget that." The banker paused a moment to think. Finally, he asked, "Those men, Flynn, where did you find them?"

"Over by Stockton."

"What was their problem?"

"No problem, boss," Flynn said. "They're just bums and cutthroats down on their luck. They'd kill their own mothers for a bottle of whiskey. They've got nothin'. I had ta supply the guns, saddles and horses, even."

"Well, it was worth the expense," Talbert mused. "Where are they, now?"

"In an old abandoned line shack, five miles north of

town," Flynn said. "Which reminds me, I'll need more money ta keep them in food and booze."

Talbert nodded. "Alright. We'll keep them handy for the next raid, if we need to. Otherwise, we'll get rid of them." Talbert stopped to think. "Ah, you didn't mention anything about me, did you? To them, I mean. Do they know about me?"

"Oh, no, boss. They got no idea who you are. They think it's all me," Flynn replied. "Just me."

"Good. Make sure you keep it that way."

"Sure, boss."

Talbert took some money from the top drawer of his desk and gave it to the big man. Flynn took it, finished his drink and put out his cigarette. He left to stay at his girlfriend's place behind the Double Down Saloon.

The banker stood up, stretched, yawned and then went through the door to his bedroom. As a bachelor, he didn't need a house. After he married Shelly Kincaid, he'd live on the ranch with her and her grandfather.

Talbert lay on his cot listening to the wind outside and thinking of the lovely Shelly Kincaid. He knew she didn't love him, not yet, but in time she would. He'd lavish her with all the things that every young girl dreamed of having, gifts of every kind. He had the money to do that, more money than he needed. He would use his money to make her see that he loved her and over time she would come to return that love. Then his life would be complete. He'd have it all, everything he ever wanted.

Talbert couldn't wait to own her, to add her to his other possessions.

5.

Jared and Marshal Richards took three horses and blankets and rode out to collect the bodies of the convicts. They started early and reached the site by noon. Coyotes were there but scattered when Jared fired a shot.

"Hell," Marshal Richards said, "there ain't enough left ta bother with. I'll write out a report backin' you up. You'll still get the reward, Jared."

Jared chuckled. "They were useful, after all. At least the coyotes made use of 'em."

He and the marshal started back.

Later, in town, Jared rode over to Ma Bradley's boarding house to see how Shelly Kincaid was doing. She was in a room on the first floor of the two-story, whitewashed clapboard building.

"I just came to see how you were doing, Miss Kincaid," Jared said. "I hope you don't mind."

"What? No flowers? Yer supposed ta bring a girl

flowers, cowboy!" She pretended to pout.

"Next time," Jared said smiling.

"Candy, too."

"Sure, candy, too."

They both laughed. He stood holding his hat, not knowing why he had come. He was already out of words to say.

"Is it snowing?" she asked. She knew it was. She wanted to keep him from going.

"Yeah. Pretty bad," he replied.

"Shit!" The word exploded from her mouth. She immediately grinned and apologized. "Sorry."

Jared chuckled, looked away for a moment, then back. She was staring up at him. For some reason she made him feel taller than the six feet high he was.

"Well, reckon I'll be going, Miss Kincaid."

"My grandfather wants you. So do I."

"I'm just passing through, ma'am," Jared explained. "I'm heading for Stockton."

"Right away? Right now?"

"No. I have to wait for the fifteen-hundred-dollars reward. The marshal said it would be ready in a week."

"Why not stay out at our place until you get it?" she asked. It was almost a plea. She looked out of the window at the falling snow. "We just lost half our men. We need help."

Jared understood that. "I guess I could." He paused a moment, then nodded. "Sure. I could do that, ma'am."

"Shelly. Don't call me ma'am. It makes me feel old."

"Alright, Miss Shelly."

"That's a little better."

They stared at each other. He shifted nervously on his feet and looked away, towards the door.

"I guess I better be goin', Miss Shelly."

"You kin kiss me before you go, if ya want to."

"No, I can't do that. Your grandfather wouldn't like it."

"That's my problem. I'll deal with him."

"No," he said and walked to the door.

Her voice stopped him.

"I won't ask agin," she said. "Think about it."

Jared had the door half open but stopped. He sighed deeply, closed it again and slowly turned to stare at her. She was staring back. He chuckled, walked to the bed and leaned down. She put her hand behind his neck and pulled his face close and kissed him. When it was over he pulled away.

"It won't mean anything to me," he said. "I'm going to Stockton, like I said."

"We'll see about that," she said. "Now, go see my Gran'pa."

Jared left. Once outside he mounted up and rode over to the jail house to see the marshal.

"I'll need directions to the Double K," Jared said.

The marshal looked at Jared and chuckled.

"What's so funny?" he asked.

"You. Yer face is all red. She kissed ya, didn't she?"

"Never mind that. How do I get to the Double K, is all I wanna know."

Fifteen minutes later Jared was riding out of Kherson's Flats in the snow, heading for the Double K Ranch and wondering why.

6.

Shelly Kincaid's grandfather stood by the kitchen window and stared out at the deep, white blanket of snow in the yard of the Double K. He could hardly see through the ice crystals that covered the glass.

"The trouble is, Jared," he said, "the darn temperature keeps changin'. The sun melts the top layer of snow in the day and then it freezes into a crust at night."

He paused to draw on his pipe. The bowl felt warm and comfortable in his right hand.

"The crust is hard and sharp as glass. When the cows try ta walk on it, it cuts their legs. They get scared and confused. Sometimes they're too afraid to move an' just die where they stand."

Jared sipped his coffee with his left hand.

"The only thing we kin do is try ta get some hay out to them," Kincaid said.

"Can't they get at the winter grass?" Jared asked.

"Nope. Not enough ta stay alive in the cold. They starve little by little."

"You could end up losing the whole herd, then."

"That's likely what's gonna happen if we don't get some feed out to 'em. And after that ambush, I can't ask the men to go to Hays City for another load. Anyway, I ain't got enough money even if they would go."

"Even if you had the hay, you don't have enough men to get it out there, especially in this weather," Jared said. "Anyway, you couldn't pull a wagon through snow this deep."

"An' it'll keep gettin' deeper," the old man said. "I suppose there ain't anything ta be done, is there? I'll jest have ta face it. I'm gonna lose it all this winter."

Kincaid walked over to the stove, poured himself another cup of coffee and refilled Jared's cup.

"How many do you stand to lose?" Jared asked.

"Fifteen thousand head. There are five of us in the valley, all about the same size. They'll lose, too."

Jared whistled. "That's, what, maybe seventy-five thousand head?"

"Thereabout."

Jared rolled a cigarette and lit it.

"You know what I'd do if I were in your situation?"

"What?"

"I'd pick up some barbed wire and fence posts and enclose an area connected to the back of the barn, a holding pen big enough to hold maybe a hundred animals. You know, like a big corral behind the barn."

Kincaid laughed. "Yeah? An' then what, pray fer rain?"

"Nope, I'd bring in twenty-five of my best and healthiest bulls and cows, run them right through the barn into that pen and hold them there for the winter. By spring, when the cows drop their calves, you'll have the start of a new herd."

Kincaid chuckled again. "How would I feed them?"

"What's the least amount of grain a cow can get by with for one day?"

"Oh, about ten pounds of high quality grain," Kincaid said. He began to think. "If I brought in ol' Hercules, my alpha bull, and some of my best stock cows an' kept them in until spring, by golly, that might leave me with enough ta start a new herd, an' that's better than nothin'!"

Jared made a quick calculation. "All you would need would be about 250 pounds of grain a day for twenty-five animals for maybe sixty days. That's a total of 15,000 pounds of grain. It should get you through the winter."

The old rancher stroked his chin, thinking about it.

"Thet's less than three sacks a day. We could buy that at the Hays City granary," Kincaid said. Then, "But, how could we get it back here? Yer talkin' about haulin' a hundred an' fifty sacks up from Hays City."

"No more wagon trains," Jared said. "And stay away from Kherson's Flats."

"There's an old coach road from Stockton ta Hays City, but it's twenty miles longer. It goes around Kherson's Flats. You kin latch on ta it five miles west of here."

"That's twenty-five miles extra," Jared said, "but I could come back that way to avoid an ambush." Jared paused to consider the possibilities. "One heavy duty buckboard could do it, one that could carry about fifteen bags."

Kincaid replied, "Sure, with a strong horse in front, it should. It's all level land, no hills."

"That makes it a lot easier." Jared said.

"It might work, Jared," the old man said. "We could bring up maybe 3,000 pounds a week." Kincaid's eyes lit up from the thought of saving his herd.

"It's worth a try," Jared said. The old man suddenly sighed and shrugged. His shoulders stooped. "What's the matter?"

"Money. I ain't got any unless I go to Talbert for it."

"Would he give you a loan?"

"I'm not sure. He'd want to know the details. He's like that. He won't make a bad loan because of the board of investors."

"Can you trust him?"

"Oh, sure. He's been good to me. An' he's stuck on Shelly, as you saw back in town." Kincaid chuckled. "Hell, if she married a banker, all my troubles would be over."

"Yeah," Jared said. "I guess they would, alright."

"I have ta tell her to say yes to him, the next time he pops the question," Kincaid said. Jared said nothing. He got up and stood by the window and stared at the falling snow.

"It's snowing pretty bad," Jared said. "Mind if I sleep in the bunkhouse?"

"Not at all. Stay as long as ya want."

"Thanks for the offer." Jared nodded and left.

Kincaid's words echoed in Jared's mind. He'd have to keep Shelly Kincaid at a distance.

It was the way the code worked.

7.

Jared took his horse down to the barn and discovered three other horses were already bedded down there. He took his mount into an empty stall and stripped it down. Next, he found an empty pail, filled it with snow and put it near a pail of grain. The horse would eat the snow when it got thirsty. Before leaving, Jared untied his bedroll and put the blanket over the horse's back.

"Stay here," Jared said, rubbing its neck.

Once outside he was hit with a blast of cold wind that drove the snow hard across the yard. He pulled his coat collar high, held onto his hat, bent low and trudged through the high drifts. After making it into the bunkhouse, Jared went to the potbelly stove to warm his hands and ears.

There were three cowboys playing cards at a table near the stove. They stared at him.

"You the one who saved Shelly?"

Jared nodded as he looked them over.

"You all that's left?" he asked.

"Yep," the one wearing his hat and coat said. "The other four lit out this morning."

Jared saw an empty chair at the table. He walked over and sat down.

"How come?"

"We ain't been paid this month," the one with a beard said. "An' with this weather the way it is, it looks like we ain't gonna be paid until the springtime."

The third one, short and stubby with a red face, said, "An' maybe not even then. This spread is finished, if ya ask me."

Jared nodded. "Yeah, it looks that way, doesn't it?"

"Anyway, I'm movin' on," the one in the hat and coat said. "I got a gal in Newton. I'm gonna stay with her until the thaw comes."

"Same here," the one with the beard said. "I'm headin' as far south as I kin get. I ain't stoppin' till I hit the Nueces."

"I'll be right behind ya, pard," red face chuckled. "I'm gonna git me one of them Mexican gals. They keep ya warm all year round."

They all laughed.

"Does the old man know you're all leaving?"

"Yeah," the beard said. "We told him yesterday. He understands."

"I hate ta leave like this, him bein' down on his luck an' all," the hat said, "but I think this ranch is dead. All of 'em are. There's gonna be sech a winter kill here that all these ranches around here are gonna lose every last cow they got. An thet's a fact!"

"Anyway," red face said, "after what happened with the wagon train, it ain't healthy around here anymore."

Jared nodded. He thought about telling them his plan but didn't. They had made up their minds so he left it at that. He made idle talk with them for a while, swapping tall tales from the past. They smoked. The hat passed around a bottle of whiskey. Before calling it a night, red face stoked up the stove. They pulled their cots up close to it and lay in their clothes with blankets over their bodies, listening to the blizzard outside. It stopped snowing a few hours before dawn.

Late in the morning they all went up to the ranch house.

Old Kincaid cooked them a last breakfast of bacon, grits, eggs and coffee. After they had eaten they said their goodbyes and rode away. Kincaid watched them go with a sad face.

"They was all damn good cowboys," he said. He paused a moment. "I'm goin' into town to see Talbert. Give it one last try."

"For a loan?"

"Yeah. He probably won't give it ta me, but I gotta do somethin'."

"Sure," Jared said. "I'll go, too."

It was turning colder. The air had a harsh bite to it as Jared saddled his horse and Kincaid hitched up his buckboard. They rode quickly towards Kherson's Flats, arriving about noon. The old man headed straight for the bank and Jared rode on to the jailhouse.

"Glad you stopped by, son," the marshal said. "I got a wire from the county seat. They're okayin' thet reward money. It'll be at the bank by Friday. I'll get it and hold it fer ya."

"Thanks, Marshal," Jared said.

"How's Kincaid doin'?"

"He's in town now, over at the bank asking for a loan."

The marshal chuckled. "He ain't gettin' a penny from Talbert unless he convinces Shelly ta marry him."

"What?"

"Yep! Hell, the whole valley knows what he's up to."

Jared didn't know how to reply, so he said, "Well, she could do a lot worse than marry a banker."

He didn't sound very convincing, even to himself.

The old lawman scratched his stubbly chin and screwed his face up into a frown. "I don't know about thet. There's somethin' fishy about him and thet Flynn fellow."

"Who's Flynn?"

"He's Talbert's personal bodyguard. You'll see him at the bank door every day, standin' there like a wooden injin, smilin' at everyone as they come in."

"I wonder why he wants to marry the girl so bad?" Jared asked.

"Why not? She's the prettiest thing around here, an' he's livin' behind that store all by himself. I guess he's jest lonely," the marshal said.

"It seems to me like she doesn't want to marry him."

"She's turned him down a few times. The whole town is keepin' count on thet." The marshal chuckled. "But he jest won't give up."

"He's pretty rich, isn't he?" Jared asked.

"Yeah. He's into investin' money an' gets a good commission on land sales, too. So he's pretty well off."

"Does he own any land himself?"

"Nope. Not one acre," the marshal said. "But if'n he marries Shelly Kincaid, he'd end up with the Double K, though."

The marshal took out the makings and built a cigarette. Jared did the same and they sat by the stove smoking and chatting.

Finally, Kincaid came riding up in his buckboard. He walked in with a big smile.

"I got the loan," the old rancher said, smiling. He patted the pocket of his coat.

Marshal Richards and Jared glanced at each other for a

moment. Both were surprised.

"Yep, once I told him the plan, he was all for it," Kincaid said. "He thought that idea of using the Stockton coach road was a darn good idea."

The marshal glanced at Jared again.

"Let's go tell Shelly," Kincaid said.

"Heck, I'll go with you," the marshal said.

The three of them walked across town to the boarding house. Shelly was sitting up in bed, reading a book and eating candy. They stood around her.

"Look, Gran'pa! Mr. Talbert has been spoiling me," she said. "He's brought me a book and a box of candy. Ain't thet nice?"

"It sure is," Kincaid replied.

Shelly went on. "An' he's asked me ta marry him agin."

"Oh? Did you say you would?"

"I said I'd give it some serious thought." She stared at Jared to see his reaction. He looked away to avoid her eyes. "What do you think I should say, Gran'pa?"

Kincaid looked over at Jared for a moment, then back to

his granddaughter. He cleared his throat.

"Well, if yer askin' me, girl, I'd say yer askin' the wrong person. I don't know how ta answer thet question. But if I did, I'd say you should look into yer heart. It'll tell ya what ta say."

The room went quiet.

"Amen," the marshal chuckled.

8.

"How is this gonna work, Jared?" Kincaid asked. "We got nobody left in the bunkhouse."

"It's a one-man operation," Jared explained. "I'll take a buckboard through Kherson's Flats to Hays City and stay overnight. In the morning I'll ride over to the granary and pick up fifteen sacks of grain and haul them back."

"Remember," Kincaid warned, "Come back on the old Hays City to Stockton coach road. Don't go near Kherson's Flats with the load. Not after what happened last time."

"Alright, I won't."

"You'll have ta make at least two trips a week, Jared," Kincaid said, "fer at least five weeks. Is it possible?"

Jared chuckled. "We'll soon find out."

"I don't know how I'm gonna repay you fer yer help, Jared."

"Heck, I ain't got anything else important to do. Anyway, the whole area has come to a stop."

The next day was clear and crisp. Kincaid gave Jared enough money for the grain and a little extra for food and an overnight stay at a Hays City hotel.

Jared got an early start and headed for Kherson's Flats. As he rode down the main street, Flynn, the big man at the door of the Kherson's Flats Savings and Loan, saw him go by. Jared waved to him, forcing a smile. Flynn watched him stop at the jailhouse.

The marshal came out to greet him.

"Flynn was looking. He seemed curious," Jared told the marshal.

"Yeah, I noticed. He was unusually curious, I'd say."

"Yeah, well, I'll see you tomorrow, most likely," Jared said.

"Alright. Good luck," the marshal said, waving as Jared got the buckboard moving.

Normally it was a six hour ride to Hays City by buckboard, but because of the snow it turned out to be eight hours. Jared stopped three times to feed the horse from the box of oats he carried on the back of the bed. By the time he rolled into the town, the box was almost empty.

He drove through town to the stables, unhitched the horse and rented a stall. He paid for a feeding and a rubdown for the animal, then walked back uptown to check into the hotel. He was so exhausted he fell asleep without eating.

The next morning Jared had a big breakfast at the town beanery, hitched up the buckboard and drove over to the granary. It was crowded and the line was long. After a two-hour wait he bought 15 one-hundred pound sacks of mixed grain and left.

Outside of Hays City he turned left onto the old Hays City to Stockton coach road. The weather held clear and he made good time. It took an hour longer but he made the trip without incident and rolled into the yard of the Double K at ten that night. He had successfully bypassed Kherson's Flats.

Frank Kincaid was ecstatic. He grabbed Jared and hugged him like a long-lost friend.

"Any problems?"

"No, but we'll need to change horses each trip. It's a long haul."

"Don't worry, I've got some big, strong ones in the corral."

"Good. And I'll need a bigger grain box. Pulling all that weight takes a lot out of 'em."

That week Jared made three trips. That gave them 45 one-hundred pound bags of grain which they stacked in a stall in the barn.

"Why don't you take a few days off?" Kincaid asked. "You looked bushed."

Jared ignored the question. "How is Shelly doing?"

"Much better. She'll be home soon."

"What about Talbert?"

"Him? He's hangin' around her like a lovesick puppy. Visits her every day with books an' sweets. It's a regular courtin' ceremony."

The following week Jared added another 4,500 pounds of mixed grain, bringing the total to 9,000 pounds. He was near exhaustion.

The one bright spot in all of it was that Shelly Kincaid would be coming home soon.

9.

"What the hell is going on, Flynn?" Talbert asked.

"I'm not sure, boss," the big man replied.

They were in Talbert's office in his place behind the store. It was late in the day.

"Well, you better find out and quick!"

"All I know is Jared is staying out at the ranch with the old man. He comes by twice, sometimes three times a week in a buckboard, heading south. He stops an' talks to the marshal and keeps going."

Talbert took a cigar from his vest pocket and lit it. Flynn waited to get his full attention.

"Go on."

"Well, I staked the boys five miles down the road south of town to wait fer him to come back."

Flynn stopped to roll a cigarette. Now Talbert waited.

"And?" the bank man asked.

"Nothin'," Flynn said with a shrug. "Nothin'."

"What the hell are you telling me? That he doesn't come back?"

Flynn nodded. "That's right. The next time I see him is when he rides through town again from the Double K."

"It doesn't make any sense," Talbert said. He thought for a moment. "Did you ever think to follow him, to see where he goes?"

"No, should I?"

Talbert exploded in anger. "Yes, you idiot!"

"Alright, I'll do that, boss."

Talbert sighed and sat down at his desk.

"Shelly will be going home in a few days," he said. "That will give me an excuse to go out there and see what's going on. The old man hasn't been in town so I don't know what he's up to. But before she goes home I want that cowboy Jared to disappear. You understand what I'm saying, Flynn?"

"You want him killed?"

"Do I have to draw you a picture?"

"No, no," the big man said.

"Alright, then, do it! I don't care how, but do it right away. I don't want him around the old man or her!"

"I'll have the boys take care of him."

"No," Talbert hissed through clenched teeth, "I want you personally to take care of it."

"Why not the boys, boss?"

"Because I don't trust them. They're misfits and garbage, that's why. If they ever find out that you and I are connected, they'll have something on me for the rest of my life."

"Oh, yeah, I see, boss," Flynn said.

The next day Jared rode through town and south towards Hays City. The sky was overcast and it looked like it would begin to snow soon.

Art Flynn sat on a buckboard behind a barn at the south edge of town, waiting. He had gotten up early and was now beginning to feel the cold. Even his gloves, heavy coat and hat weren't keeping him warm. He was used to the easy life. Standing at the door of the bank day after day had turned him soft.

Finally, he heard noises and a buckboard came rolling by. It was Clay Jared.

"I've got you now, slick,' Flynn muttered.

He waited a few moments until Jared was out of sight on the southbound road and then pulled the buckboard out to follow. He hurried at first but when he saw Jared at a distance he slowed down, staying well behind to avoid suspicion.

"Where the hell are you going, Jared?" Flynn said out loud to himself.

The hours passed slowly and the sky above stayed heavy with gray clouds. Jared stopped once, then again hours later, to feed his horse. Flynn had brought no food, and his horse began to tire. It was about to drop from hunger when they rode into Hays City seven hours later.

Flynn was not prepared for such a long trek and had not eaten in all that time. He was cold, drained and exhausted.

He stayed out of sight as Jared drove his buckboard down to the stable. After Jared left, he dropped his buckboard there, too, and followed the cowboy uptown to a beanery. He waited in agony, his mouth watering for want of food, until Jared came out. Flynn followed him again, this time to the hotel. It was easy because of the large crowd of people, wagons and horses on the street.

He stood outside until he was sure Jared had gone up to his room, then went into the lobby to the reception desk.

"I'm supposed to meet an old friend here," Flynn told the desk clerk.

"What's yer friend's name, mister?"

"Jared. Clay Jared."

The clerk looked at the register and nodded. "Yeah, he just signed in. Room eight, second floor."

"Thanks," Flynn said.

The big man nodded and walked from the foyer to the stairs and then up to the second floor. He located the room, came quietly back down and went quickly over to the beanery where he ordered a steak smothered in onions, fried potatoes and baked beans. Then he had a piece of apple pie and a cup of coffee.

He felt much better now and sat thinking about how good life was under Greg Talbert. All things said, the real estate man and banker had been good to him. He never wanted for anything, clothes or food. Even women. No, Talbert had been his savior. Sometimes he was short tempered, but that didn't bother Flynn. He knew who buttered his bread.

Flynn was feeling good when he left the beanery and went to a nearby saloon. It was dark and crowded so he squeezed in between two cowboys and ordered a whiskey.

"Still snowing out?" the cowboy on his left asked.

"No," Flynn said.

That was the end of the conversation. Flynn finished his drink and was thinking of leaving but ordered another one. He suddenly felt a bit on edge.

He hadn't killed a man close up in a long time and hadn't quite figured out how he was going to kill Jared. Should he kill him with a knife or gun? He had both. Maybe he should strangle him, or suffocate him with a pillow while he slept. Would the door be locked or not? Those thoughts rolled around in Flynn's head as he drank his fourth shot of whiskey.

Time seemed to drag. Around midnight, Flynn left the bar. He had drunk quite a lot and his legs felt rubbery as he walked back to the hotel. No one was at the desk. Holding onto the bannister, Flynn made his way up the stairs, under the glow of the oil lamps hanging above.

Once on the second floor landing he went slowly down to Jared's room. When he got there, he reached into his coat pocket, got his knife and folded out its six-inch, razor-sharp blade. He listened at the door for a few moments then took the knob in his hand and turned it very slowly. The door almost opened on its own, as if inviting him in.

Flynn smiled and stepped into the room. He stood staring at the bed where Jared lay completely covered. Not even his head showed.

In one quick movement, Flynn leaped upon the bed and stabbed away. Again and again he drove the long blade into the body below. He kept doing so until he realized there was nothing there to stab except a rolled carpet.

"What the hell?" he muttered.

"Hi, Flynn," a voice said behind him.

As he turned to lash out with the blade, a hand came out of the darkness holding a rock. It smashed Flynn on the right temple so hard, it crushed his skull in. He fell across the bed.

Jared checked for signs of life and found none. He wiped the rock clean on the bed covers, shoved it into his saddlebag and put on his mackinaw.

He quietly left the hotel and walked quickly down to the stables. After tossing the saddlebag into the boot well of the buckboard, he gathered up a pile of straw and made a bed in the back of the box. Finally, he wrapped himself up in a blanket and lay there shivering on the straw, listening to the wind blowing hard between the empty stalls.

It started to get colder. Jared remembered the sign in the beanery window saying it was open all night. He sat there drinking coffee and eating crullers until the crack of dawn, then went back to hitch up the buckboard.

10.

Two hours later Jared left the granary with another fifteen sacks of mixed grain. In another hour he was back on the old coach road to Stockton.

As he looked ahead, he saw the tracks of wagons and coaches that came out of the towns and villages heading south into Hays City or north to Stockton. Jared knew that ten miles to the north was the newer road from Stockton, through Kherson's Flats and south to Hays City.

That was the road where Jared had seen the Double K wagon train ambushed. It saved twenty miles, but Jared wasn't trying to do that.

But now that Flynn was dead, Jared wondered what Talbert would do. What would his next move be?

Jared's mind wandered. What was the banker's game? What was he after? Were he and Flynn connected or had Flynn been working on his own? Talbert seemed to have a special interest in the Double K spread, and Jared now knew why. The answer was Shelly Kincaid. Once he had her, he had the Double K, too.

The snow had slacked off, but coldness dropped in behind it, settling like a heavy, frigid blanket that sucked the air from the lungs of animals and humans alike. Jared pulled his coat collar higher and his hat lower.

Time passed slowly. Jared stopped to feed the horse and let it rest. He tied a blanket over its back then started out again. Two more stops and night began to close in. Jared could see the wagon tracks that ran ahead of him like black lines on a strip of white.

Suddenly the buckboard gave a bounce and a shudder and leaned to the left. It felt as if it was dragging something behind it or had taken on more weight. Jared stopped and jumped down to take a look.

Of the four wheels on the bed of the buckboard, the rear outside wheel was completely gone. Jared looked around and saw it lying in the middle of the road twenty feet behind.

Upon close inspection, Jared saw that the keeper pin had dropped out, allowing the axle nut to work loose and fall off. Once the nut was gone, the wheel had slid off, too.

The buckboard let out a groan as the weight of the grain

kept downward pressure on the rear of the bed. If the wheel wasn't put back on soon there could be damage. As it was, the load was starting to lean and tilt towards the road.

Jared immediately went to work removing the bags of grain, lifting the hundred-pound grain sacks out of the bed and dropping them in a pile on the side of the road. It was hard work and he wished he had brought along a bottle of whiskey to cut the cold from his bones.

When he had half of the bags unloaded from the rear, he stopped, thinking it wasn't necessary to remove the weight from the front wheels. Those grain sacks could stay there.

He walked back to the wheel, set it upright and examined it. It seemed okay and rolled good. He brought it back to the buckboard and put it in position in front of the axle hub. He quickly saw it didn't line up. The hub hung six inches too low, and that presented a problem. This was a job for two men, not one. He needed to lift the back of the wagon to raise the hub up six inches so he could slide the wheel onto the axle and screw on the nut.

Jared thought about digging a ridge in the road but abandoned that thought. The road was frozen rock solid. He tried lifting the back of the wagon but didn't have the strength to get it more than two inches higher. Even if he could get it high enough someone else would have to put the wheel in place.

Jared stood by the side of the buckboard looking round, hoping to see a light somewhere. All he saw was a white landscape below and blackness above.

Jared chuckled. This would have been the last trip he'd need to make. Here he was, stuck helpless in the middle of nowhere on a black, cold night. And it was getting colder.

His luck had finally run out.

11.

Before settling down in Kherson's Flats, Greg Talbert was a lowly bookkeeper in a large investment firm in New York City. The firm was housed in a three-story, red-brick building on the upper east side of Manhattan.

An employee's importance in the firm depended on what floor he or she worked on. Executives worked on the top floor, managers worked on the second floor and accountants worked on the first floor. If you were a lowly bookkeeper, however, you worked down in the basement, which is where Talbert worked.

For seven long, tedious years, Talbert worked in the damp, musty basement of Geist, Vanvought and Sneller. His job was to record financial transactions by posting amounts for sales and expenses in ledgers. It had been exciting at first but soon became redundant and boring.

As for a social life, Talbert had no close friends except a boyhood school companion named Art Flynn.

Flynn was not very bright, and Talbert, for the most part,

did all of Flynn's thinking for him. Flynn was a bully at school and protected Talbert from all the other bullies. By the time they completed high school, the two were inseparable friends, and Talbert kept Flynn close to take care of any enemies. Flynn seemed to enjoy bashing people around.

While working at his bookkeeping job, Talbert managed to support himself and Flynn. They lived together in a cold water flat in the city and were as close as brothers.

When Talbert got a promotion to payroll clerk, he stumbled upon an opportunity he never expected. He found it easy to siphon off small amounts of money into dummy accounts he had set up after reading about it in the newspapers.

The practice was called by various names such as check kiting or lapping. It amounted to shifting small amounts of money around several times until it ended up where Talbert wanted it, which was in several small, secret accounts he had set up in and out of state.

Technically, it was called embezzlement but the police simply called it stealing. It had to be done skillfully so as not to attract attention.

Talbert started out moving small amounts at first, just to test the waters. When he didn't get caught, he got bolder and more skillful. His supervisors didn't seem to even notice the clean looking clerk in the fifth row of the huge bookkeeping section. He never was late for work and never caused trouble. Most times they didn't even remember his name.

One day Talbert put in his notice. Even then, no one seemed to care, not even his fellow workers. He was such a boring person they were glad to see him go. When one curious fellow clerk asked him where he was going, he said he was going south.

Instead of south, Talbert took a train west with his personal body guard, Flynn, and a briefcase containing over a dozen bank books, each with a separate personal account in a dozen different banks in Chicago, St. Louis and Kansas City. He also had stock shares from investing in various companies in the cattle trade in those same places.

Talbert was looking for a small, remote town where he could settle down and be respected as an honest, caring businessman. He visited several small towns along the Kansas Pacific railroad and accidently heard the name Kherson's Flats mentioned as an up and coming place for investment.

Once there, he met with the town council and various businessmen and laid out a proposal to save the failing Kherson's Flats Savings and Loan, a small, struggling bank that made small, unsecured loans to the local farmers and ranchers. It was mostly a mom and pop bank.

When they accepted his offer, Talbert was thrilled. He had finally gotten to a place where he was seen as a very important person. Something he had dreamed of while working in that damp basement in New York City.

Within a year, the bank was doing very well, and so were Talbert's investments. He kept his eye peeled for any opportunities that might develop. He opened a small real estate office just to show people he was a solid citizen with the town's interest at heart and that he was there to stay.

One opportunity in particular caught his interest. It was a small ranch run by a pretty young woman named Shelly Kincaid. Called the Double K Ranch, it was owned by her grandfather, Frank Kincaid.

When Talbert first set eyes on pretty Miss Shelly he decided he would end his many years of being a bachelor. The young woman would make him a fitting wife and he would become a gentleman rancher as well as a real estate agent and a bank manager. That would make him a very important person in Kherson's Flats.

To that end, he was very gracious and polite to Shelly and her grandfather. He played the gentleman well, doing small things to please her, waiting for the proper time to propose marriage. Very soon Talbert wanted the lovely Miss Kincaid more than anything he'd ever wanted in his life.

And things were going very well until a cowboy named Jared came along.

The same day Talbert sent Flynn to kill Jared, Talbert drove his buckboard out to the Double K Ranch. It was a difficult fifteen miles with the wind blowing the snow around in blinding gusts. He took with him a box of expensive imported French chocolates shipped in from a confectioner in St. Louis.

He pulled into the Double K yard in the afternoon on an overcast day. He tied his buckboard at the rail and climbed the porch steps in his expensive fur coat and hat. Shelly had seen him arrive and met him at the door. They went into the warmth of the kitchen.

Talbert handed Shelly the candy and said boastfully,

"Chocolates, Shelly! Imported from France, my dear!"

"Why, thank you, sir," Shelly replied, smiling. She put the box on the table.

"Come an' sit, Mr. Talbert," Kincaid said. "Take a load off yer feet, sir."

The banker sat down at the table across from Shelly's grandfather and said, "How are you, Frank?"

"A bit on the frosty side, but all told I'm fine."

Shelly poured Talbert a cup of coffee and then took the lid off the box of candy. Talbert looked around the room.

"Nice cozy place you have here, Frank."

"Thank you, Mr. Talbert," Kincaid said. "Shelly-girl keeps it up. Without her it'd be a mess, I'm afraid."

Talbert sipped his coffee, picked out a piece of candy and bit into it. He nodded. "Very good. Try one, Shelly."

"Later tonight, after supper, Mr. Talbert," Shelly said.

"How are you doing with those grain shipments you told me about, Frank?" the banker asked, casual like.

"They're comin' along just fine, Mr. Talbert," Kincaid replied. "We got most of it. In fact, Jared went to Hays City fer the last load this morning. He should be comin' back in a few hours."

"Well, I'm glad I was able to help you with that loan, Frank."

"And I thank you for that, Mr. Talbert. Without that loan we'd be plumb outta business."

"It's the least I could do. The board fought against it but I demanded they let it go through."

"And I'm really grateful, sir. I sure am," Kincaid said. "I'll pay you back this spring for sure and that's a promise."

"You know, Frank," Talbert said, looking directly at Shelly, "if your granddaughter would do me the privilege of becoming my wife, you wouldn't have to pay a penny of that loan back."

The old man looked at his granddaughter. She looked away. There was a cold silence.

"What do you say to that?" Kincaid asked Shelly.

"To what?"

"Mr. Talbert just asked you to marry him."

"That's not what I heard," Shelly said calmly.

Kincaid laughed. "No? Then, what in tarnation did you hear, girl?"

Shelly stared down at her hands and shrugged.

"Well, the last time he asked me, it sounded like a proposal, but this time it sounded more like a threat."

A tense quietness fell over the room broken only by the crackling of the fire in the kitchen stove. Talbert's face began to turn red. He fought for control and forced a smile, looking at Shelly.

"I'm sorry, I didn't mean it that way," he said. He paused then said, "Will you marry me, Shelly?"

The young girl looked at her grandfather. Talbert didn't see old Frank's eyes speaking silently to her, telling her not to be afraid, to follow her heart.

Shelly stood up and stepped over to the stove with her back to Talbert.

"You've been most kind to us, especially me, Mr. Talbert," she said. "An' I thank you fer all you've done, sir. But I'm not intendin' ta get married just yet."

It was not so much her choice of words, but how she said it that brought home to the banker how far apart their worlds were. She was a plain and simple girl of the West. So was her grandfather and that cowboy, Jared.

Anger rose within Talbert. Who was this girl to refuse him? He wanted to elevate her in life and she rebuked him. Any woman in town would have jumped at his offer.

His anger was churning inside him. He wasn't going to let her off that easy.

"But you must have known how I felt about you by now," he said angrily. "I've made it clear, haven't I!"

Shelly shrugged her shoulders. "I thought you were just bein' nice an' friendly-like," she said, "you bein' so much older than me."

Those words cut deep. Talbert jumped up off his chair. "Oh, I see! You think I'm too old for you, is that what you're saying?"

Shelly turned to face Talbert.

"I didn't mean that."

"Oh, yes, I think you did!" Talbert said coldly.

"I'm sorry, Mr. Talbert," Shelly said. "I really am."

"Oh, you'll be much sorrier in the coming days," the

banker said. "I'll make sure of that!"

Frank Kincaid slowly stood up and faced Talbert.

"Maybe you'd best go, Mr. Talbert," he said calmly, but firmly.

"Oh, indeed I will, Frank!"

Talbert grabbed his hat and rushed outside, slamming the door as he went. He ran towards the buckboard, slipping on the cold icy ground and landing on his knees. He groaned in pain as he struggled to his feet and climbed onto the buckboard. The seat was covered with snow but he sat on it anyway, cursing to himself. He yelled at the horses, snapped the reins and rode away.

12.

Talbert was furious. Shelly Kincaid had humiliated him in front of her grandfather and she must be made to pay dearly for that. As he rode back to Kherson's Flats, the banker searched his mind for a way to hurt her.

An hour later he was back in his room behind the real estate office, drinking bourbon and thinking of a way to bring her down hard.

By now, Flynn should have taken care of that pest Jared. He couldn't wait to hear Flynn tell about it. He could visualize it already, Flynn grabbing Jared by the throat and choking him to death, or better yet, clubbing him senseless with his fists. He regretted not being there to see it happen.

But the Kincaid girl had to be taught a lesson, put in her place. Who did she think she was? She should suffer for what she did. She was nothing but a poor as dirt, stupid cowgirl with no education. He was better off without her. Actually, she had done him a favor by making him realize what a fool he had been. He could see things clearly now.

But Talbert couldn't put it aside. The more he drank and thought about how she had treated him, the angrier he got. Something had to be done to her now, not tomorrow or the day after, but now, right away. She was back there at the Double K laughing about how she had snubbed his proposal of marriage. Her and old Kincaid were splitting their sides laughing.

The worst cut would be when the town heard about it!

Talbert made a decision right then and there to take action on his own. He got back in the buckboard, drove down to Roy Sanders' mercantile, bought food and whiskey and headed out of town to the old, deserted line shack where Flynn's men were.

As he pulled up he saw five horses tied to a makeshift rail. There was a light on inside, and he could hear them talking about Flynn. They were wondering why he hadn't come to see them in the past few days.

Suddenly two men came out of the shack with their guns drawn.

"Who the hell are you, mister?" one growled, waving his gun in Talbert's face. For a moment the banker feared for his life.

"I'm a friend of Flynn's," Talbert managed to say, trying to sound calm. These men looked like the killers Flynn had said they were.

"Where the hell is he?" the other one growled. "We're almost outta grub an' whiskey."

For a moment Talbert wasn't sure why he was there. But it was too late to turn back now.

"I've got some here, in the back," Talbert said, pointing. They grabbed the food and whiskey out of the buckboard and took it into the shack.

Talbert got down off the bench and followed them in.

The only light in the shack came from a fire that burned in the remains of a broken fireplace. The rickety roof had been patched up to keep out the snow. A wooden box served as a table. Empty whiskey bottles lay scattered about. Straw and smelly blankets lay in the corners. The place was rank with the stench of tobacco juice and unwashed bodies.

These were five of the meanest, filthiest men Talbert had ever seen, right out of the pages of a penny dreadful.

The leader came over to Talbert and sized him up.

"What happened to Flynn? Why isn't he here?"

"I sent him out on a job," Talbert said. "He works for me."

"Yeah, well, why the hell are you here?"

Two of the men were tearing hungrily into the smoked ham, cutting it into slabs. The others worked on opening the bottles.

"I've got another job for you and your men, if you're interested."

"Maybe. Let's hear it."

"Can we talk over there, in private?"

Talbert walked over to the farthest corner. The outlaw followed. The banker explained what he wanted done to the Double K.

"We don't kill women," the leader said.

"What do you usually do?"

"You know. Have a little party. We take turns, if ya git my drift."

Talbert chuckled. "Very good. To some women that's worse than being killed, I'd imagine."

Talbert pulled a roll of money from his coat.

"Here's a thousand dollars. It's yours. Share it as you see fit with your men. You'll get another thousand when the job is done. Is that a deal?"

The outlaw stared at the money for a moment and looked over at his men who were eating and drinking. They didn't look back. He took the roll of bills, stuck it in his pocket, then glanced quickly over his shoulder to make sure they hadn't seen him.

They hadn't noticed.

"What's your name?" Talbert asked casually.

"Daggs," the outlaw replied.

"Alright then, Daggs," Talbert said. "I guess we're in business."

Daggs chuckled. "I guess we are."

"Good," Talbert said. He took a piece of paper from his other coat pocket and gave it to Daggs. "Here's a map showing where the Double K is. Look at it after I'm gone."

The outlaw nodded and put it in his shirt pocket.

"I'd wait until after midnight. Catch them in their sleep. It's just the two of them," Talbert added.

"Consider it done, boss," Daggs said.

Talbert smiled. Suddenly he felt powerful. Here was this big killer calling him boss. It was the power of money. With enough money you were in control. You could make things go your way or any way you wanted them to go. No one could stop you if you had money. Those with money always came out on top.

As for that little bitch, Shelly Kincaid, she would be brought down and humbled in a way she would never forget. He would like to see the look on her face after Daggs and his men got finished with her! She wouldn't be so snotty and uppity after they worked her over. No, she'd be glad if he even looked at her.

Suddenly he felt very good about himself. He couldn't wait to see the look on Flynn's face when he told him what he had accomplished while he was off killing Jared.

What the banker didn't realize was that he was being followed.

After he had left, Daggs had mounted up and rode after him, staying back far enough as not to be seen. When Talbert pulled up behind his real estate office, the outlaw was in a stand of pine trees fifty feet away, watching him unlock the door and go in.

Just to make sure, Daggs walked his horse quietly through the alley alongside Talbert's real estate office and around to the front. He read the sign above the door, chuckled and rode quickly back to the old line shack.

When Daggs got there he stood in the yard and rolled a cigarette. As he smoked it, he began thinking of the whiskey and the painted ladies he could buy with the money Talbert had given him.

13.

As he stared up and down the road, Jared clapped his hands and pounded his feet on the frozen road, trying to keep warm. For the past hour he'd seen nothing but a deer and a fox running across a nearby field.

By some quirk of luck, after searching about on the road, he'd found the axle nut and keeper pin. All he needed now was help to get the wheel on. And that wasn't likely to happen. No one in his right mind would be on this lonely road this late at night without a good reason.

The wind picked up and wailed for a few minutes. As it died down he thought he heard someone singing. It sounded more like a frog croaking more than anything else. For a moment he figured it had to be the wind playing tricks on him. Then, suddenly, there was movement down the road, coming fast in his direction. A big hulk emerged, clattering out of the dark. It came fast, making an awful racket and was quickly upon him.

He jumped to one side to avoid being crushed.

It was a big hauler, the kind used to carry loads of corn and produce, with high sides. Two men sat up in the box drinking. It went thirty feet beyond Jared before the six-horse team stopped.

One of the men leaned over the side and yelled down at him.

"You havin' trouble, pilgrim?"

"I sure am," Jared yelled back against the force of the wind.

"Could ye use a little help, there, friend?"

"I sure could, friend!"

"Be ye Christian or heathen?"

"A drinking Christian," Jared yelled.

"So be we all," the man said and dropped over the side of the wagon. He walked up to Jared and handed him the bottle. He was the biggest man Jared had ever seen.

"God bless you, friend," Jared chuckled and took a long, hard pull on the bottle.

"I figured ye be a might dry," the man said, laughing.

"Not any more, thanks to you," Jared said, handing the

bottle back. The man stuck it in the coat of his sheepskin mackinaw.

"I see you dropped a wheel, lad."

"That I did," Jared said.

"Well, then, let's get the bugger back where it belongs." He called to his friend. "Brother John, come give us a hand."

The other man crawled down off the wagon and joined his friend.

"You stand aside, pilgrim," the second man said. "Let us handle this."

Within a half hour they had the wheel back on and the keeper pin back in place. The man with the bottle offered Jared another drink and the cowboy took a second pull. It burned warm and good all the way down.

"Where you headed?" Jared asked.

"Utah," the second man replied. "Salt Lake area."

"Thanks for your help and God speed you on a safe journey," Jared said.

"And you, too, friend."

They climbed up on the big wagon and with a crack of

the whip sent the team up the road. Jared lifted the grain sacks back in the box, fed the horse again and then started out, following the tracks made by the haulers.

Two hours later he saw where they had turned left at the fork that would take them in the direction of Colorado. Jared kept going straight until he came to another fork. He turned right and heaved a sigh of relief. The Double K was only one more hour away. The horse must have sensed it was close to home. It laid its ears back and surged forward.

They were half a mile from the Double K when Jared heard a popping, intermittent sound.

At first he wasn't sure what was making it, but as he drew closer he recognized it for what it was, gunfire. He stopped the wagon at the bottom of a rise, got his rifle from the boot well of the buckboard and ran up to take a look. Down below he could see the flash of rifles by the fence of the Double K.

After studying the scene, he spotted five men lined up along the fence. They were pouring round after round into the ranch house. All of them seemed to be either drunk or having a good time, or both.

One yelled, "Come on out, old man! Meet yer maker!"

Another one let out an Indian war cry, and another followed that with an insane cackle. In between shots they passed a bottle of whiskey along the line.

"Come on out girl, I ain't gonna hurt ya! I jest wanna make love to ya! Haw!"

"Yeah, we're jest a bunch a lovers, is all!"

"Don't be bashful little darlin', come on out!"

Someone in the house returned fire, hitting one of the attackers. The outlaw lurched up and over the fence, into the yard.

"Damn! Hey, Daggs, they got Tobey!" one of them yelled. "The sonsabitches! I'm gonna kill them all!"

The man leaped over the fence and started to charge the house. Jared quickly aimed and fired off a snap shot. The shot went true and caught the outlaw on the run with a bullet to the chest. He went tumbling head over heels into the snow and lay still.

Jared levered off one more shot and the third outlaw grunted, threw his arms up and flipped backwards into the snow with a bullet to his head.

One of the two remaining outlaws yelled to his

companion.

"What the hell's goin' on, Daggs?"

"We're bein' ambushed, Ned! Thet sonofabitch Talbert sent us into a trap!"

Jared held his fire as the two remaining attackers retreated into the trees where their horses were tied. Moments later they rode away.

There was an eerie silence.

"Is that you, Jared?" Kincaid yelled from the house.

"Yeah. They're gone. I'm comin' in!"

Jared got back in the buckboard and drove it around the ridge and down into the yard.

He rushed into the house and found Shelly in the front room by the window. She was behind an overturned table that had been splintered by gunfire, just sitting there with a rifle in her lap, looking afraid and exhausted. The windows of the room had all been shot out. The walls were full of bullet holes.

She looked up at Jared and forced a weak smile.

"I'm sure glad you got here," she said. "I'm plumb outta

bullets."

"Where's your grandfather?"

"Gran'pa's over there."

She pointed to where Frank Kincaid sat in a corner holding his shoulder. A gun lay on the floor nearby.

Jared went quickly over to him.

"Is it bad?"

"Hell, I've been shot worse than this," the old man said.

"Where's the medicine box?"

"I'll get it," Shelly said. She got up and hurried into the kitchen.

"Who the hell were they?" Kincaid asked.

"They were sent by Talbert," Jared replied. "I heard one mention his name."

Kincaid tried to laugh. "Jesus! All Shelly did was refuse ta marry him! He didn't have ta kill us over thet, did he!"

Jared shook his head in wonder. "I guess not, unless he's plumb loco."

Shelly came back with the first aid box, and she and

Jared attended to the wound in her grandfather's left arm. The bullet had cut a bit of flesh away but it wasn't severe. In a few minutes Jared had it cleaned and wrapped.

"Thanks fer jumpin' in, Jared," Kincaid said. "You saved our skins, an' thets fer sure. I was all outta bullets. How many did ya plug?"

"I got two. Shelly got one."

Suddenly the girl groaned and slumped over. Jared caught her before she fell. Her face was pale and damp.

"My side. I took one in the right side," she said, trying to smile as if it was nothing.

Jared laid her gently on the floor. In the darkness he felt for the blood and found where the bullet had hit.

"I'll have to open your shirt."

"Sure. I ain't bashful." Her voice was weak.

Jared saw where the bullet had gone straight through just below her ribs. She had lost some blood. He got a cotton pad from the box, poured some alcohol on it, cleaned the wound and placed a gauze pad over it. Finally, he wound a bandage around her waist.

"You'll have to see the doc again."

"This is the second time you saw me shot."

"Yeah," he said. "Don't make a habit of it. I might not be around the third time. It's not as bad as the last one. Now you've got one on both sides."

"Ain't I the lucky one."

"It's not funny," Jared said.

"Kiss me, I'm dyin'," Shelly said.

"No, you're not."

"I am, too."

"You're a big faker."

Jared kissed her lightly and then picked her up in his arms. He carried her upstairs to her bed.

"Are you hungry?" he asked.

"No. Tired. Just let me sleep."

He covered her with blankets and went back downstairs. Kincaid was in the kitchen lighting an oil lamp. He put it on the table and went to stoke the fire.

"Let me do it," Jared said, and took over.

"Is she gonna be alright?" Kincaid asked.

"I think so. I'll go get the doc out here in the morning."

Kincaid made a pot of coffee and they sat at the table drinking. Jared rolled a cigarette.

"Talbert is an evil man," the old rancher said.

"He's a dead man," Jared replied. "I'm going to kill him."

After he had finished with his coffee and cigarette, Jared got up.

"I'll take care of the horse. It's been damn good."

"I'll go with ya," Kincaid said.

"No. Get some sleep. I'll settle the horse in and leave it at that. I'll unload the grain in the morning."

"Alright."

Jared went outside and drove the buckboard into the barn. As he unhitched the horse he thought about what had happened in the past day and a half. Flynn had tried to kill him, and Talbert had hired men to kill the Kincaids.

Talbert had a lot to answer for and Jared vowed to see that he did.

14.

Daggs was very angry. And so was Ned. They believed that Talbert had set them up to be ambushed. Which, if he had taken time to think about it, wouldn't have made any sense. Why would Talbert hand him a thousand dollars to have him kill the old rancher and his granddaughter and then hire someone to kill him, too?

But, by Daggs's twisted logic, it made perfect sense. Talbert didn't want any witnesses. The banker had told him that he had sent Flynn on a job but as Daggs saw it, it was Flynn who had fired on them from the ridge above the ranch house.

"Here's how I see it, Ned," the outlaw chief said. "Thet bastard Talbert planned to have Flynn kill us all, then go in an' finish off the girl and the ol' man, an' make it look like we did it."

Of course the theory was full of holes but not in Daggs's mind. Nor did he really care about his men. It was that second payment of a thousand dollars that he was after. Now he wouldn't have to split it five ways.

After leaving the Double K Ranch, Daggs and the man called Ned rode into Kherson's Flats. The town was asleep at this late hour. Daggs remembered where Talbert's real estate office was. Ned followed him around back and they tied their horses in the stand of pines behind the place.

Talbert, who was a light sleeper, heard someone at the door and thought it was Flynn returning. He quickly went and opened it.

The last thing he saw was the knife blade in Daggs' hand.

After that, he saw nothing.

15.

The morning after the attack, Jared loaded the bodies of the three dead outlaws on the back of the buckboard. They were frozen stiff from lying all night in the snow. Their horses had wandered down to the barn to forage for hay. He tied them to the back of the buckboard and rode slowly into Kherson's Flats.

He stopped at Doc Edmund's place first and told him about Shelly and her grandfather being wounded.

The doctor nodded and said, "I'll go out there this morning."

Jared thanked him, left and took the bodies of the three outlaws down to the marshal.

"What the hell's this?" the marshal asked.

"These jokers attacked the Kincaid place. Shelly got one and I got two. Two others got away," Jared said.

"I guess those horses belongs to these three?"

"Yep. They should pay for the burial, if you sell them."

The marshal sighed and nodded.

"Come on, we'll take the bodies down to Lester the undertaker so he kin make the boxes. I'll have 'em buried out in the cemetery with the rest." He chuckled. "Lester needs some action. It's been dull in his area lately."

They found the undertaker's place between the Double Down Saloon and the stables, down from the doctor's office. It looked more like a carpenter's place than an undertaker's parlor. Sawdust and wood shavings were all over the floor and empty pine boxes were piled near the walls.

"We do the ceremonies up at the church," Lester explained upon seeing the look on Jared's face. "Except in charity cases like this where we jest stick 'em in the ground and forget 'em."

After they had unloaded the bodies into pine boxes, Jared and the marshal went back to the jailhouse.

"I'll sell the horses and gear and give the money to Lester," the marshal said. "They should bring five hundred apiece, at least."

Jared thought about telling the marshal about the killing of Flynn but decided to hold off until another day. Nor did he say anything about Talbert possibly being involved. He'd wait to see what developed.

Jared left and drove the buckboard back to the Double K Ranch. Doc Edmunds was just leaving.

"They're gonna be just fine," the doctor said on the way out.

Jared waved and yelled, "Thanks, doc!"

Three days later, Marshal Richards rode out to the Double K Ranch. It was midafternoon and the snow had slacked off. He sat in the kitchen drinking coffee with Jared, Shelly and her grandfather, huddled around the big iron stove.

"I want Greg Talbert arrested, Marshal," Kincaid said.

"I can't arrest him, Frank."

"Why not?"

"Because he's dead."

"Dead?"

"Yep. When he didn't show up at the bank two days ago, one of the clerks went over to where he stays behind his real estate office and found his body."

"Yer kiddin' me, Fred," Kincaid said.

"Nope, I ain't, Frank. He was stabbed ta death and robbed. Whoever did it took every penny they could find."

"How sad," Shelly said.

"Any ideas about who did it?" Jared asked.

"Somebody thinks it was some nasty looking fellahs who were stayin' out at the line shack north of town. I took some men out there ta question them, but they was gone."

"What about his friend, Flynn, the one he had guardin' the bank? Maybe he killed Talbert," Kincaid said.

"Thet might be," the marshal said, "but Flynn is gone, too."

Jared cleared his throat. "I can clear that up marshal."

"Alright, son, go ahead. I'm a-listenin'."

"Remember how you had a suspicion about Flynn?"

"Yeah. So?"

"Well, you were right. He attacked me in Hays City. I killed him. You can wire the marshal there. They've probably found his body in my hotel room by now and the knife he was going to kill me with."

The marshal squinted and nodded, scratching his chin.

"So I was right, then. But what was he up to?"

"I asked myself that same question. That, and who ambushed the wagon train last month. For me, it all points to Talbert and Flynn. I think they were behind it. I know he was behind the attack on the Double K two nights ago. One of the attackers yelled out his name," Jared replied.

"Talbert, you say? Why Talbert? How does he fit in?"

"Mr. Kincaid told him about the plan to send me to Hays City to get the grain by buckboard. No one else besides you, me, Shelly, Mr. Kincaid and Talbert knew of the plan."

"So yer sayin' that Talbert told Flynn an' sent him ta ambush you?" The marshal thought about that for a moment. "Thet does sorta make sense, doesn't it?"

Kincaid spoke up. "When Shelly refused to marry him two days ago, he got real mad an' threatened us."

"Yeah," the marshal said, his face lighting up. "It all fits. The same men who attacked you two days ago also attacked the wagon train. They were working for Talbert, but Flynn was doing the dirty work. He hired them and Talbert provided the money. That's how I see it."

"He wanted Shelly and her grandfather at his mercy so he could have her and the ranch," Jared said.

Marshal Richards nodded and said, "Well, it all blew up in his face, I reckon." He sipped his coffee. "The reason I came out here, Frank, is ta tell you the ranchers are holding a meeting tonight at eight at the Cattlemen's Association Building in town."

"What for?" Kincaid asked.

"They're gonna talk about the weather situation an' things. It's said a winter kill is a-comin' on soon. If thet's so, it'll be the end of you ranchers unless ya figure a way out."

"Alright, we'll go," Kincaid said. "We'll all go, Jared, Shelly an' me."

The marshal got up and stretched.

"I kin feel it in my bones, Frank," he said. "It's a-gonna be a bad one."

The marshal was about to bid them good day when he stopped and took a brown envelope from his coat pocket. He chuckled and handed it to Jared.

"I almost forgot. Another reason I came out is to give you that fifteen hundred-dollar reward."

The marshal took a piece of paper from his pocket, unfolded it and laid it on the kitchen table. Jared picked it up and read it.

"Do you have a pencil?" he asked Shelly.

She nodded and got a pencil from the cupboard. Jared signed the receipt and handed it back to the marshal.

"Fifteen hundred," he said and dropped the envelope on the table.

Jared nodded and stuck it in his shirt pocket without checking it. He stood up and shook hands with the marshal.

The marshal tipped his hat to Shelly and turned to Kincaid.

"Oh, Frank, Roy Sanders, the new bank manager, said ta tell you yer credit is good at the bank fer as long as you need it."

"Tell Roy I said thanks, Fred."

"I will," the marshal said and left.

16.

After the marshal left, Jared hauled in firewood and stacked it in the wood box next to the big cast iron stove. There wasn't much else to do except try to stay warm. They drank coffee, ate Shelly's sourdough biscuits covered with sausage gravy and watched the wind drive billows of snow across the yard and into the field beyond the deserted bunkhouse.

Later Shelly got out the cards and they played poker for matchsticks, listening to the wind howl outside. Around late afternoon it stopped snowing and the wind died down.

"Well, let's get ready ta go to the big pow-wow," Kincaid said.

"I wonder what it's all about?" Shelly asked.

"We'll soon find out, girl," her grandfather replied.

Jared looked at Shelly with concern. "Maybe you should stay home and rest."

"I'm fine," Shelly said. "We'll take the buckboard an'

you'll keep me warm, won't ya, kind sir?"

Jared glanced at Kincaid. "Is she always this pig-headed, Mr. Kincaid?"

Frank chuckled. "She takes after her ma. Once she gets a notion ta do something there ain't no stoppin' her. There ain't no way ta stop her short of hog tyin' her to her bed."

It was still light when they piled into the buckboard and headed for Kherson's Flats. Kincaid put his rifle wrapped in a blanket behind his feet in the boot well.

"Ya never know about them damn wolves," he said.

The snow had stopped and it was getting colder. Shelly sat bundled up between the two men. She held Jared's right arm and laid her head on his shoulder. They didn't talk much.

It was dark by the time they rode the buckboard down the main street of town to Colby's stables and left it there under his care. Jared gave him a double eagle to feed and water the horse and they walked around the corner to the big, red Cattlemen's Association Building. It was already packed with ranchers sitting in chairs, waiting for Tory Nesbit of the Flying N to start things off. Finally, he took the floor.

"Men, the reason I called this meeting is because it looks like we're gonna git hit real hard with a winter kill an' we need to plan for it."

"What can we do?" one rancher asked. "I'm new here. I just bought the Circle T this past summer. I'm originally from New Jersey. I sure would appreciate some good advice on what ta do. There's nothing in my book covering this sort of thing."

Someone chuckled. "One of them carpetbaggers from the East, huh? Welcome to our world, friend. Haw!"

Another man spoke up. "Hell, I got enough hay ta last at least for a month. If there's a thaw by then, the spring grass will show through. I don't see the need ta do anything."

Old Tory Nesbit shook his head.

"You ever been through a winter kill, Mr. Simon?"

"Nope. Sure ain't."

Nesbit looked around the room until he saw an old, bent over, silver-haired man.

"Lew, tell Mr. Simon what a winter kill is. He doesn't seem ta understand."

The man named Lew stood up on bent legs.

"Sure. Be glad ta, Tory." His voice was high pitched like a rusty gate swinging in the wind.

The old man paused for a moment, staring off into the distance, arranging his thoughts. He looked down at his hands for a moment, then looked up.

"I was jest a young cowboy when, the summer before the winter kill, we had a long dry spell. It hardly rained at all. Maybe once or twice, I can't really recall whether it did or not. If it did, it didn't amount to much. The grass broke in pieces when ya walked on it. It sounded like glass was cracklin' under yer feet. I'll never forget that sound as long as I live."

Old Lew looked down again to inspect the palm of one hand.

"This was back in 'fifty-five. Some a-you weren't born yet, but yer gran' pappies would remember, fer sure."

Lew sniffled and wiped his nose. He looked past the staring faces, into the distance as if seeing it all over again.

"Well, an early frost hit. It was so early, it seemed ta throw nature off balance. It killed any grass and trees that had survived the drought. After the frost, the snow came in.

It snowed hard fer two, three weeks straight."

Someone yelled out, "What's yer point, old man?"

Lew didn't seem to hear.

He went on. "The snow was so deep we couldn't git any hay out to the herd. If we had tons of hay it wouldn't have mattered. The snow had us boxed in. Five feet deep. An' when the sun did come through, it made things worse."

There were chuckles and snickers.

"How come?" someone shouted. "Thet don't make no sense ta me."

"Thet's because yer stupid," old Lew shot back. "It put a glaze on top of the snow and at night thet glaze froze ta ice. Ice hard as a rock, ya dumb asses!"

Lew now had their attention.

"The wind blew so cold it dropped the temperature to thirty below zero. It blew from late December to the middle of February. It was so bad, people died from the cold. When the snow finally melted enough, we got back in the saddle an' rode out. An' that's when we saw it."

Lew stopped here. His voice had cracked and he had to swallow hard to clear his throat.

Finally, someone asked, "Saw what, old man?"

"The winter kill." He stopped to wipe his nose again. "There were dead cattle fer as far as the eye could see. It looked like a huge carpet of dead fur. A sea of carcasses laid over the land. We rode for miles and miles and never came ta the end of it. Finally, we gave up an' rode home."

They were quiet now, hanging on every word.

"As it got warmer, the stench of rottin' meat spread out on the wind, covering the land. Just the smell alone made ya sick. Buzzards came by the thousands to feast on the dead beeves. The wolves came, too, an' fought the buzzards over the meat. Carcasses came floatin' down the streams, rolling along like driftwood, the big, black birds standing on them and eatin' as they floated along. The water stunk an' wasn't fit ta drink. It was like ridin' through a bad dream only it was real."

Old Lew stopped. He seemed in a trance, staring blankly over their heads at some vision only he could see.

"Thet's horse shit, ol' man. You been drinkin' too much red eye. There never was no winter kill and there ain't gonna be none," a young rancher's son said with a sneer.

Arguments broke out. Accusations began to fly. Tory Nesbit called for order but no one paid any attention to him. Suddenly a big rancher came up alongside him and shoved Nesbit aside.

He yelled for attention and got it.

"Go home, everybody," he bellowed. "This is a waste of time. There ain't gonna be no winter kill, an' thet's a fact. Accordin' ta the Farmer's Almanac, this is gonna be a mild winter an' the Almanac is a lot smarter than Tory Nesbit!"

Men began getting up and leaving the building, first by twos and then by groups. Jared, Shelly and Frank walked over to where Nesbit and six ranchers stood talking to one another.

"Nice try, Tory," Kincaid said.

Old Nesbit shrugged. "I guess there are only a few of us who remember, Frank."

Frank nodded.

"Yeah, most of them came into the valley later, after we'd lost our herds an' were ready to call it quits," one of the ranchers said.

"Well, I'm afraid they're gonna learn a lesson they'll

never forget," Nesbit said.

Jared looked around. The big room was almost empty but for the small group gathered around Tory Nesbit.

"Mr. Nesbit," Jared said. "I'm Clay Jared, the new ramrod at the Double K. Our men left us high and dry. Could you spare a few of yours?"

"Sure," the old rancher chuckled. "They're jest sittin' around twiddlin' their thumbs an' playin' cards, an' hopin' it'll snow forever so they don't have ta go ta work. How many ya want?"

"Four would do," Jared replied. "For about three months. I'll pay them the same as you do."

"Sure. I'll send ya four of my best men. Keep 'em as long as ya need 'em."

"Whatta ya up to, Jared?" one of the other ranchers asked.

Jared explained his plan to bring in some blood bulls and cows before a crust formed on the snow and fence them in for the winter.

"I was gonna suggest somethin' like thet to them block-heads before they left," Nesbit said.

"Well, you had better move quick before a crust forms," one of the ranchers replied. "Once it does, the horses will balk. They won't go near it. It'll cut their legs up good."

Nesbit rubbed his stubbly chin and nodded. "You know, Jared, I kinda like this plan of yours. It would work a lot better if we all got in and pulled together."

"How many do ya think will jump in with us?" Kincaid asked.

"I figure we kin get maybe nine or ten at least," Nesbit answered.

"Exactly how would it work?" someone asked.

They looked at Kincaid. He looked at Jared and nodded.

"It might work this way," Jared said. "You wire in an area connected to the rear door of the barn. Make it big enough so fifty or more cows and bulls have room to move around in. Leave the rear door open and the front door shut. It's that simple."

One of the ranchers looked doubtful. "So ya put a three strand wire fence in back of the barn and corral half a hundred head of beeves and bulls? How ya gonna feed 'em?"

Jared explained how he had brought up the grain from

Hays City. "If we get ten of us working together, we can stockpile enough grain to last through until the thaw."

"Hell, we already got 15,000 pounds stored in the barn," Kincaid said.

"I ain't got no money fer that much grain," another rancher said.

"The new bank manager, Roy Sanders, says he'll help us," Kincaid replied. "We keep goin' until the spring thaw and then all ten of us will combine our bulls, heifers and calves into one big herd and take 'em out to range."

"Are you talkin' about formin' a combine, Kincaid?"

"If ya wanna call it thet, sure. Why not? We'll call ourselves the Kherson Valley Cattlemen's Combine. How's that sound?"

Old Nesbit chuckled. "It sounds good ta me, Frank."

The others all nodded.

"Ya got my attention, Kincaid. Let's go down to the beanery and knock out the details," one of the ranchers suggested. "I think better over a hot cup of coffee."

"Good idea," Tory Nesbit chuckled.

They all went out into the night feeling good.

17.

The Double K Ranch and nine other small ranchers formed a caravan of buckboards and made a twice weekly run to the Hays City granary. Those that didn't have the money were given loans from the Kherson's Flats Savings and Loan Bank.

In between trips they worked on the barbed-wire enclosures, connecting them to the rear of their barns. The four men from Tory Nesbit's spread, the Circle N, worked well, and they had the fence up in no time.

One day Kincaid took Jared aside.

"Jared, yer usin' yer own money ta pay fer the wire an' them cowboys, aincha?"

"Yes. So what?"

"Why are you doing it?"

"To save the Double K."

"Is it Shelly?"

"She's part of it."

Kincaid looked troubled.

"Then I gotta tell ya up front, I got plans fer her. Do I need to say more?"

Jared caught the old man's meaning right away.

"No, Frank, I get yer drift."

"No hard feelin's?"

Jared nodded. "No hard feelin's. I hadn't planned on settlin' down permanently, anyway."

"Then, we'll shake on it?"

"We'll shake on it," Jared said and shook Frank Kincaid's hand.

With the enclosures finished, there was only one thing to do, and that was to go out and bring in the blood bulls and the cows. It was a combined effort with all the ranchers joining in. One at a time, the cowboys rode out into the wind and waist-deep snow to find the herds. They found them gathered in large groups. The wind had pushed them together and they stood huddled in large masses.

It wasn't easy to pull them apart. They fought back.

Some of the animals were already in bad shape. A few lay dead. Getting at the bulls was a hard job. They refused to budge and tried to keep the cowboys away from the cows. Some had to be lassoed and dragged through the snow, snorting and charging at the horses. Usually the sound of a gun would start the herd on a stampede, but not now, not in this weather. They were half starved, confused and scared.

It was slow, difficult work made harder by the blinding snow and cold. The temperature was dropping more and more each day. Some days they could only get a dozen or more beeves in from a distance of sometimes twenty miles and more. It was punishing work that went on from dawn until dusk.

It took twenty-five days straight, without a break, to get the job done where each spread had their quota of bulls and cows. Soon after that, the sun came out for a day, and the snow formed a thick crust that night. Man and beast were locked in place and at the mercy of nature.

"By golly, we did it, men!" Frank Kincaid boasted.

It was Christmas and Jared and the four cowboys from Nesbit's spread sat at the kitchen table enjoying the warming heat from the big stove. Shelly had spent the last few days cooking. Pumpkin and apple pies were lined up on the cupboard shelf. Jars of spiced apple cider sat on the table. A big pot of beef stew bubbled on the cast iron stove.

"We got 'er done jest in time," one of the cowboys said.

"Yeah," another said. "Thet winter kill you talked about? Well, I reckon it's here."

That day, Jared paid them their month's wages and they rode into town to get drunk.

The first week in January there was a sudden, sharp drop in the temperature. The wind stiffened up and blew the soft layer of snow away, bringing the ice crust to the surface. The loose snow piled up in slanting drifts against the barn and down into the root cellar under the house.

Jared took the ten horses out of the corral and made stalls for them in the barn. He put a blanket over each one. Shelly took pails full of snow, melted them on the stove and took it out to the horses.

"What about the cows?" Shelly asked.

"They'll eat snow," Jared replied. "They'll see a bull do it and then they'll do it. Don't worry."

By the middle of January, the temperature averaged

about seventeen below zero in the Kherson's Flats area. Few people ventured out into the cold except old Doc Edmunds. January was a busy month for babies.

Business picked up at George Kelly's butcher shop. Hunters and trappers brought in rabbit, pheasant, wild turkey and woodchuck, and Kelly bought everything they had, skin and all. He hung the pelts in the window for sale along with the skinned animals. Skunk fur turned out to be popular, although the butcher did not sell the skunk meat.

On the ranches that had joined the combine, there were plenty of cow chips to burn in the stoves, and the cows and bulls were able to move in and out of the barn freely to eat at the grain troughs.

Luckily for the Double K, Shelly had helped her mother with the root cellar under the house. A door in the hallway led down a set of wooden stairs to it, seven feet into the ground.

It had a goodly supply of potatoes, waxed turnips, carrots, onions, winter and summer squash. Some of it was preserved in jars on wooden shelves, vegetables such as shredded white and red cabbage, pickled cucumbers, red, yellow and green peppers, and some dark green chili peppers.

Dried pole beans, peas, apples, apricots and pears hung from strings tied to the rafters above.

There were also slabs of salted beef and pork and sealed jars of peach preserves.

One day in the kitchen, Jared talked about it.

"Your mother was a very smart lady," Jared said.

Shelly's eyes moistened a bit. "Yes, she was."

"Her root cellar is going to save our lives."

"Every spring an' fall, she and I would spend hours in the kitchen an' down there in the root cellar. She showed me how ta cook and preserve stuff. I miss all that. I was nine when she died."

"How did they pass?" Jared asked, trying to approach the matter delicately.

"There was a lung sickness going around, but I didn't catch it. It was nine years ago. Gran'ma died of it, too. Jest me and Gran'pa made it through."

"I'm very sorry."

"Yeah, me, too," Shelly said. "I sure miss her a lot."

The temperature dropped down to twenty below zero and held like that until the middle of February, then suddenly rose. The snow melted quickly and there was flooding. Eventually the dry earth absorbed it, leaving puddles and ponds where green algae formed. The cold had killed off the mosquito larvae, but the horseflies emerged by the millions. The fields of red earth lay naked and dead.

One day in late February, Jared, Frank, Shelly and the four cowboys rode out to see the damage. They took their rifles and extra ammunition.

The few cattle that had somehow survived lay on their sides, mere skeletons with their stomachs bloated. When they heard the people coming, some of them made mournful, pitiful sounds and tried to rise up. But they couldn't.

Jared and the rest sat in the saddle and shot them until they ran out of ammunition.

The dead cattle lay as far as the eye could see in every direction. The smell of rotting corpses burnt the lungs. One of the cowboys vomited and got so sick Jared had to send him back to the ranch.

In this vast sea of dead cattle, a ritual of nature was being performed. Buzzards by the thousands circled high in the air above. Every second, one would swoop downward. When it got three feet above the ground, it would fold its wings and drop onto a carcass and begin to eat the rotting flesh. In some places there were two or three buzzards to a carcass. In other places, four or five of the black flesh-eaters tore in a frenzy at the putrid remains. The red heads stuck out against the ocean of black, bobbing and pecking as they gouged away.

Behind all this was the humming of the wings of millions of horseflies that came to join the feast. When they sensed humans and horses were near, many of them turned for a meal in their direction.

This usually sent Jared and the rest riding back to the ranch as fast as they could.

18.

It took another year for nature to adjust the balance and repair the damage it had inflicted on living things. The buzzards were gone, leaving a strange landscape of skeletons picked clean by animals and insects and bleached white by the sun.

Strangely, the prairie grasses, the wheat grass and wild rye, the switch grass and others, all came back greener, yellower and taller than before. The nutrients of dead cattle carcasses and buzzard waste had combined with the melting snow to form an elixir of life that stimulated growth as never before. The prairie very quickly bloomed yellow, green, gold and red again.

The ten ranchers of the Kherson's Flats Cattle Combine branded their cattle with a KFCC brand and took their small herds out into open graze under the watchful eye of the cowboys. It was estimated that in two years they would have a large herd and would be making a profit.

The cold grasp of the winter kill had been broken.

But Clay Jared was afflicted with another kind of fever. It was a fever that cowboys caught from time to time. It snuck up on them when things got too calm, too easygoing. It was a fever that struck in the night when they lay on their cots or out in the line shack or sleeping on the ground. Sometimes it came upon them as they sat in their saddles out in the vast loneliness of the range with their minds wandering.

Early one fine spring morning when everyone was asleep, Clay Jared packed his gear, mounted up and rode out. He rode slow and quiet, torn between going and staying. That was the hardest part, tearing up the roots that had newly formed. It hurt and it always left a little scar on his heart.

Because of this hurt, he had learned not to look back.

About five miles out, Jared stopped to dismount at a stream by a stand of birches and let his horse drink. He soon heard the sound of pounding hooves coming his way. Jared knew who it was. She rode up and slid out of the saddle. He kept his back to her but she grabbed his arm, spun him around and glared at him.

"Thet's a damn dirty trick yer pullin', cowboy!" He looked down at the ground, avoiding her eyes. She was crying. "You sonofabitch, yer runnin' out on me, aincha?"

"You know the code as well as I do. Anyway, Frank has better plans for you."

"I don't care about the code. It can't give you what I can give you. Just reach out an' take it."

Jared shook his head violently. He looked agonized, tortured.

"Don't say things like that! You're killing me!" He sighed and calmed down somewhat. "I told you right off that kiss didn't mean anything."

"You're lyin', Jared!" Shelly yelled. "Look me in the eyes and tell me it didn't mean anything!"

Jared looked at her. They stared at each other for a long time, not saying anything.

"You saved my life, Jared! You own me! I'm yers!"

"I can't betray him," Jared finally said. "Frank said he has plans for you. I can't betray him, Shelly. Don't you see that?"

Suddenly she knew that the code had come between them. It was the rancher's right to choose what trail his offspring were to ride. It had always been like that.

Shelly dried her eyes and gave him a blank look.

"Alright, then go! I hate you! I hope you die!"

Jared forced a smile. "That's better."

Shelly suddenly came at him, slapping his face. She kissed him hard and then pulled back, looking into his eyes with a devilish smile. A moment later she was riding hard back to the Double K.

As Jared stood there watching her go, he put a finger to his mouth. It came away with blood where she had bit him.

He chuckled. "You little rascal!"

He mounted up and rode west under a clear, blue sky.

The End

A Note from the Author

Thank you for reading my book. Would you please consider rating and reviewing it? I'd enjoy your feedback. Thank you!

Western books by R. Annan

Quick Draw Westerns

Fight for the Lazy M
The Red Bandana

Jack Cordell Westerns

The Gunfighter in Winter
Long Ride to Hell's Kitchen
Owl Hawks
Gunfight at Barfield Springs
Shootout at Sanctuary City
Last Days of a Gunfighter

Clay Jared Westerns

Copperhead Moon
Cowboys of the Box R
Prisoners of Brimstone Pass
Range War in C Minor
Devil Wind
Showdown at Wamego Falls
Lightning Riders
Winter Kill

Coming Soon: Jesse Garnett Westerns

Coming Soon: Cody Brent Westerns

About The Author

R. Annan is a seasoned and traveled author with many interests. As a career serviceman he served in Korea and Vietnam. He also completed a one-year course at the Defense Language Institute at Monterey, California, and graduated from the University of South Florida with a B.A. in Art and Art History. After taking a two-year course in screenwriting at the Hollywood Scriptwriting Institute, he established The Old Time Radio Club Time Machine as both a scriptwriter and an actor.

As a young boy growing up in the city, R. Annan never passed up a chance to see a western movie. His heroes were Buck Jones, Johnny Mack Brown, Wild Bill Elliot and John Wayne, to name a few. As an adult he often wondered where his love of westerns came from. Perhaps it has something to do with his grandfather, John L. Annan, who was a cowboy from Helena, Montana, in days of old.